SQUARE
FISH

An Imprint of Macmillan Children's Publishing Group

Based upon the animated television series "My Friend Rabbit," © 2007–2009 Nelvana Limited.
All related designs, illustrations, characters and their distinctive likeness © Nelvana Limited.
Nelvana and Corus are trademarks of the Corus Entertainment Inc. group of companies. All rights reserved.

Used under license by Macmillan Children's Publishing Group.
Published in 2013 by Square Fish. Printed in China by Toppan Leefung Printers Ltd., Dongguan City,
Guangdong Province. For information, address Square Fish, 175 Fifth Avenue, New York, NY 10010.

Library of Congress Cataloging-in-Publication Data Available

ISBN 978-1-250-01662-1 (hardcover): 10 9 8 7 6 5 4 3 2 1
ISBN 978-1-250-01661-4 (paperback): 10 9 8 7 6 5 4 3 2 1

Book design by Patrick Collins/Véronique Lefèvre Sweet

Square Fish logo designed by Filomena Tuosto

First Edition: 2013

myreadersonline.com
mackids.com

This is a Level 1 book

Lexile 220L

my Friend Rabbit
and the
Snow Geese

Don't miss the
My Friend Rabbit
TV series

Based on the characters from
Eric Rohmann's
Caldecott Medal-winning picture book
My Friend Rabbit

**SQUARE
FISH**

Macmillan Children's Publishing Group
New York

It was the first day of winter.
Rabbit and Mouse
hopped over to visit
the Gibble Goose Girls.

The Gibble Goose Girls
were asleep.
Their nests were covered
in snow!

"Wake up!" said Rabbit.
"Come see your first snow."
The Gibble Goose Girls
popped up.

"Snow is so soft!"

"So sparkly!"

"So shiny!"

"So . . . everywhere."

"Should we go explore?"
asked Amber.

"But our nests are safe!"
said Jade.

"You can't stay there forever,"
said Mouse.

"Let's go!"
said the Gibble Goose Girls.

"Let's go swimming,"
Coral said.
They went to the pond.

But the pond was
under the snow.
The water had turned to ice.

"Ice is hard."

"It's not nice."

"You can't paddle in it."
"Make it melt!"

"Winter is not fun,"

said the Gibble Goose Girls.

Then Mouse had an idea.

Mouse and Rabbit
cleared off the ice.

"Whee!"
Rabbit and Mouse
slid across the ice.

The Gibble Goose Girls
watched.

"We could try."

"It seems okay."

"Looks like fun."
"Wait for me!"

"Whee!"
The Gibble Goose Girls
slid across the ice, too.

"Let's do that again!"

They slid across the ice
all morning.

"Ice is fun," said Amber.
"You can't slide on water."

Later, they went sledding.

"You can't go sledding
on grass," said Pearl.

They made a snowman.
"You can't build snowmen
with rain," said Coral.

"Now we like winter—
a lot," said Jade.